Dwayne

For Sam Day - A.S.

To Carla and Vera - M.O.

HODDER CHILDREN'S BOOKS
First published in Great Britain in 2018 by Hodder and Stoughton

Text copyright © Andy Stanton, 2018
Illustrations copyright © Miguel Ordóñez, 2018

A CIP catalogue record for this book is available from the British Library.

ISBN: 978 1 444 93344 4

1 3 5 7 9 10 8 6 4 2

Printed and bound in China

Hodder Children's Books
An imprint of Hachette Children's Group
Part of Hodder and Stoughton
Carmelite House, 50 Victoria Embankment, London, EC4Y 0DZ

An Hachette UK Company
www.hachette.co.uk
www.hachettechildrens.co.uk

ANDY STANTON

MIGUEL ORDÓÑEZ

Hodder
Children's
Books

GOING TO THE VOLCANO

Going off with Jane-o
to look at the **volcano!**

Going off with Jane-o to look at the **volcano!**

Walking down the lane-o
to look at the volcano!

Walking down the lane-o
to look at the **volcano!**

Riding the Great Dane-o

Riding the Great Dane-o

Sitting on the train-o
to look at the **volcano!**

Sitting on the train-o
to look at the **volcano!**

Jumping on the plane-o
to look at the **volcano!**

Jumping on the plane-o
to look at the volcano!

Flying off to Spain-o
to look at the **volcano!**

Flying off to Spain-o
to look at the **volcano!**

Splashing through the rain-o
to look at the **volcano!**

Splashing through the rain-o
to look at the **volcano**!

Going up the crane-o

to look at the
volcano!

Climbing down
the chain-o
to look at the
volcano!

In a lot of pain-o
because of the volcano!

In a lot of pain-o
because of the volcano!

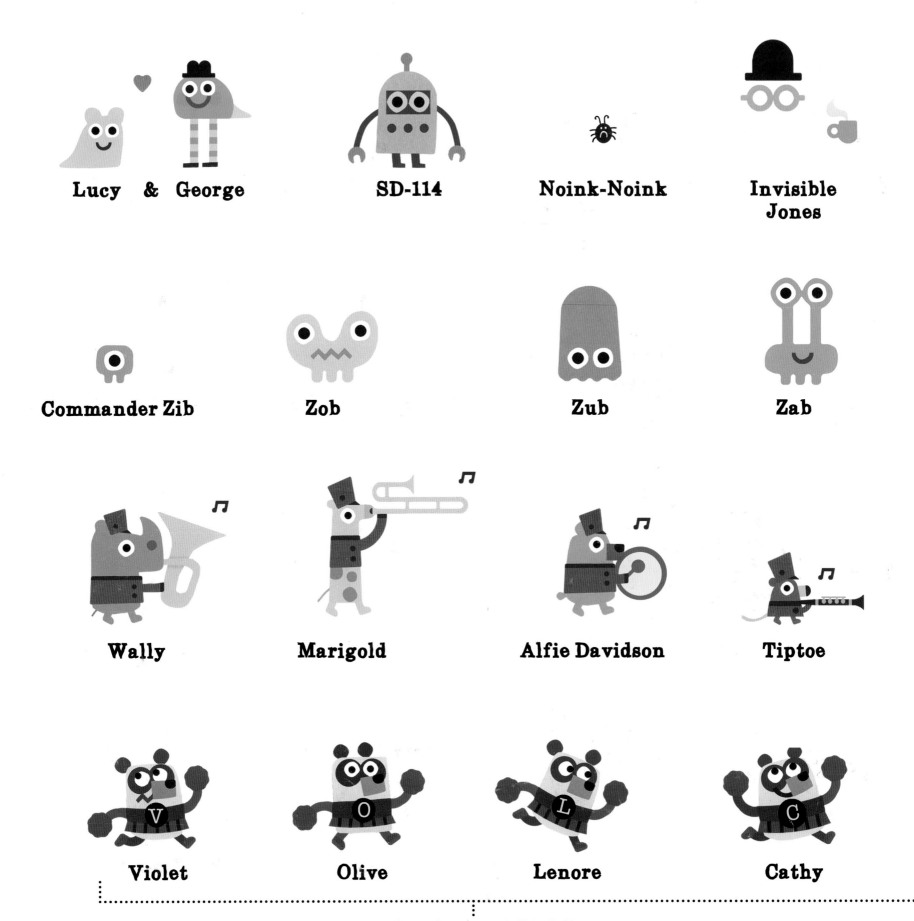

Lucy & George

SD-114

Noink-Noink

Invisible Jones

Commander Zib

Zob

Zub

Zab

Wally

Marigold

Alfie Davidson

Tiptoe

Violet

Olive

Lenore

Cathy

THE LAVA GIRLS